A
Charlie Brown
Christmas

 LITTLE SIMON

An imprint of Simon & Schuster Children's Publishing Division

1230 Avenue of the Americas, New York, New York 10020

Copyright © 2001 by United Feature Syndicate, Inc. All rights reserved.

PEANUTS is a registered trademark of United Feature Syndicate, Inc.

All rights reserved including the right of reproduction in whole or in part in any form.

LITTLE SIMON and colophon are registered trademarks of Simon & Schuster.

Manufactured in the United States of America

First Edition 10 9 8 7 6 5 4 3 2

ISBN 0-689-84608-8

Adapted from the works of Charles M. Schulz

A
Charlie Brown
Christmas™

By Charles M. Schulz
Adapted by Justine and Ron Fontes
Illustrated by Paige Braddock
Based on the television special produced by
Lee Mendelson and Bill Melendez

LITTLE SIMON

New York   London   Toronto   Sydney   Singapore

Snowflakes floated in the crisp, pine-scented air. The wind carried the joyful sounds of jingling bells, Christmas carols, and people wishing one another happy holidays.

The greatest time of the year was finally here! Whipping across a frozen pond, the Peanuts gang was as happy as, well, children at Christmastime—all except good ol' Charlie Brown.

"I think there's something wrong with me," Charlie Brown told Linus. "I just don't understand Christmas. I like getting presents, sending cards, decorating trees, and all that. But I always end up feeling sad."

Linus sighed. "You're the only person I know who could turn a wonderful season like Christmas into a problem. Maybe Lucy's right. Of all the Charlie Browns in the world, you are the Charlie Browniest."

Charlie Brown felt even sadder when he opened his empty mailbox. "Rats! Nobody sent me a Christmas card today. I know nobody likes me. But why does the holiday season have to rub it in?"

Charlie Brown felt so depressed, he decided to see his psychiatrist, Lucy. He dropped a nickel in her can and sighed. "I just don't understand Christmas. Instead of feeling happy, I feel sort of let down."

"You need to get involved!" Lucy exclaimed. She knew just how to get her patient into the Christmas spirit. "How would you like to direct our Christmas play? I'll meet you at the theater."

Charlie Brown decided to give it a try. After all, things couldn't get much worse.

On his way to the theater, Charlie Brown passed his dog. Snoopy was decorating his doghouse with heaps of shiny ornaments.

"What's going on here?" Charlie Brown asked.

Snoopy showed him a flyer.

Find the true meaning of Christmas. Win MONEY, MONEY, MONEY.
Enter the Christmas lights and display contest!

"My own dog has gone commercial," Charlie Brown wailed. "I can't stand it!" He was sick of all the greedy buying and selling that had become Christmas.

Helping his little sister, Sally, write a letter to Santa only made Charlie Brown feel worse.

"I have been extra good this year, so enclosed is an extra-long list of things I want," Sally began.

"Good grief!" Charlie Brown's stomach hurt. What had happened to giving and sharing?

"Or perhaps you should just send money," Sally concluded. "I would prefer tens and twenties."

But Charlie Brown did not have time to lecture Sally about the meaning of Christmas. He had a show to direct! He hurried to the theater.

"Let's get down to work," Charlie Brown told the cast. "It's the spirit of the actors that counts, the interest they show in their director. Am I right? I said, 'Am I right?'"

But nobody was listening. They were all dancing to Schroeder's bouncy piano music.

Ba-ba-da-ba ba-da-ba-bum-daaa-dum.

"Stop the music!" Charlie Brown shouted. Then he told Lucy to hand out the scripts and costumes.

"Do innkeepers' wives have naturally curly hair?" Frieda wondered.

Pigpen promised to keep a clean inn.

Sherman complained, "Every year I play a shepherd."

Snoopy agreed to be all the animals—even some that weren't in the play!

Lucy came up with five good reasons for Linus to learn his lines and "get rid of that stupid blanket!" But Linus found a way to keep his blanket in the show.

The rehearsal went about as well as one of Charlie Brown's baseball games. Frieda worried that Pigpen's dust was ruining her curls. Lucy called for a lunch break. Linus hid under his blanket.

And instead of listening to their director, everyone danced to Schroeder's jazz.

Ba-ba-da-ba ba-da-ba-bum-daaa-dum.

Frustrated, Charlie Brown finally cried out, "That does it!"

Lucy stopped snapping her fingers and asked, "What's the matter, Charlie Brown?"

"This Christmas play is all wrong!" he wailed.

Lucy tried to calm him. "Let's face it. We all know Christmas is just a racket set up to make people buy lots of stuff they don't need."

Charlie Brown shook his head. "This is one play that won't be like that. We need the proper mood. What we need is . . . a Christmas tree!"

"That's it, Charlie Brown! We need a great, big, shiny aluminum tree!" Lucy exclaimed. "You get the tree. I'll handle this crowd," she said, taking charge of bossing everyone around.

"I'll take Linus with me," Charlie Brown said. "The rest of you can practice your lines."

"Get the biggest aluminum tree you can find, maybe painted pink!" Lucy added.

Charlie Brown felt a familiar knot in his stomach. "I don't know, Linus. I just don't know," he said, sighing as the two boys walked to the Christmas tree lot.

Soon they were surrounded by a fantastic forest of fake trees. Some were plastic or pink or even polka-dotted!

"Gee, do they still make wooden Christmas trees?" Linus wondered aloud.

Then Charlie Brown pointed to a tiny tree barely strong enough to hold on to its needles. He said, "This little one seems to need a home."

Linus worried about what Lucy would think. But Charlie Brown bought the tiny tree anyway.

"What kind of tree is that?" they shrieked when the boys got back to the theater with the scrawny tree. "You were supposed to get a good tree!"

"You're hopeless, Charlie Brown, completely hopeless," Violet scolded.

Everyone laughed at the skinny tree—even Snoopy!

Charlie Brown's heart sank. "I guess you were right, Linus. I shouldn't have picked this little tree. I guess I really don't know what Christmas is about," he wailed. "Isn't there anyone who knows what Christmas is all about?"

"Sure, Charlie Brown. I can tell you what Christmas is about."

Linus stepped into the spotlight and said: "And there were shepherds, abiding in the field, keeping watch over their flock by night. And the Angel of the Lord came upon them and said, 'Fear not: for behold, I bring you tidings of great joy. For unto you is born this day a Savior, which is Christ the Lord.' And there was with the angel a multitude of heavenly hosts praising God and saying, 'Glory to God; peace on Earth, good will to men.'

"That is what Christmas is all about, Charlie Brown."

Suddenly, Charlie Brown didn't care what anyone thought of him or his tree. He finally felt happy, the way he was supposed to feel at Christmas!

Charlie Brown stepped out into the cold, silent night and looked up at the twinkling stars.

"Linus is right. I won't let all this greed spoil my Christmas. I'll decorate this little tree and show everyone it really will work in our play."

Charlie Brown took a bright, red ball off Snoopy's prize-winning doghouse. He hung the ball on the tiny tree. The tree slowly bent over until its top touched the ground.

That was all it took to spoil Charlie Brown's mood.

"Argh! I've killed it! Everything I touch gets ruined!"

Charlie Brown walked away with his shoulders as bent as the little tree's trunk.

After Charlie Brown had left, the others found the tree.

"It's not a bad little tree, really," Linus said. He wrapped his blanket around its base. "It just needs a little love."

The rest of the gang helped. In a flash Snoopy's doghouse decorations had transformed the tree.

The children gathered around the pretty little tree and hummed "O Little Town of Bethlehem."

They could almost see the shepherds guarding their flocks by night.

When Charlie Brown returned to the group, he could hardly believe his eyes.

"What's going on here?" he shouted.

How had the tree become so beautiful? Charlie Brown's heart filled with joy when he realized what everyone had done for his tree. It was a Christmas miracle.

Linus, Lucy, and the rest of the gang smiled and shouted, "Merry Christmas, Charlie Brown!"
And for Charlie Brown, it truly was the merriest Christmas ever.